DOCTOR · WHO

DECIDE YOUR
DESTINY

BBC CHILDREN'S BOOKS
Published by the Penguin Group
Penguin Books Ltd, 80 Strand, London, WC2R 0RL, England
Penguin Group (USA) Inc., 375 Hudson Street, New York, New York 10014, USA
Penguin Books (Australia) Ltd, 250 Camberwell Road, Camberwell, Victoria 3124, Australia.
(A division of Pearson Australia Group Pty Ltd)
Canada, India, New Zealand, South Africa
Published by BBC Children's Books, 2007
Text and design © Children's Character Books, 2007
Written by Davey Moore
10 9 8 7 6 5 4 3 2 1
ISBN-13: 978-1-40590-345-5
ISBN-10: 1-40590-345-7
Printed in Great Britain by Clays Ltd, St Ives plc

DOCTOR·WHO

DECIDE YOUR DESTINY

The Corinthian Project

by Davey Moore

The Corinthian Project

1 | 'You get used to the constant thrum of machinery when you live in an artificially-controlled environment,' says the Doctor.

'Like the TARDIS,' adds Martha, in case you have no idea what he's talking about.

But the noise inside the TARDIS reminds you of someone constantly breathing out — like a sigh that goes on forever. What you can hear now is more like the hum, rattle and shudder of an old refrigerator. Standing here in pitch darkness, this is not a reassuring sound.

And there's a distinct smell. It reminds you of the time you took a trip on a ferry — ozone mixed with some sort of fuel. And, maybe, a hint of... fish. Perhaps you're close to the sea.

'Any minute now,' says Martha, 'one of us is going to find a light...'

Bright lights snap on overhead.

'Switch.' Martha finishes, unnecessarily.

'Voice activated lights,' chuckles the Doctor. 'Cool!'

You guess that voice activated lights means it's some time in the near future — but where are you? Just a few minutes ago you were on your way to the corner shop to buy your favourite magazine. You stopped to help a young woman, whose carrier bag had split, pick up her shopping from the pavement.

You offered to help carry her groceries but she said she was going the other way to you. You were watching her walk off down the street when you realised one of her apples had rolled into the gutter. It didn't looked too bad, so you chased after her — just in time to see her stepping into a weird, blue, wooden box...

And the rest — as they say — is history. That is, if travelling to the future could be considered history. You found out that the woman who likes apples is called Martha. The blue box is a space and time machine called the TARDIS. And the TARDIS is piloted by a chap known as the Doctor, who promises to get you back to the corner shop before your magazine sells out... just as soon as you return from wherever you are now.

Looking around, you see you are surrounded by: large, padlocked leather trunks; sample trays filled with butterflies and leaves; wooden tea chests, packed with straw and overflowing with books; a giant lump of rock... and a stuffed fox. You realise you were about to stumble into the fox and shudder at its lifeless glass eyes.

'Who would keep all this junk?' says Martha.

The Doctor shrugs. 'Someone who misses their homeland,' he says. 'Or maybe just... land.'

You jump as the Doctor shouts, 'Door!' And, with a gasp, like the sound of a truck using its air brakes, a circular door slides open.

You lead the way into a wide corridor with curved, white walls. A quick glance behind you reveals the name of the room you have just left: Storage Pod C.

To turn left, turn to 32. To turn right, turn to 3.

2 You pick up Jolla's weapon. You were right, it is a water pistol! You burst out laughing. You were afraid of a water pistol!

You squeeze the trigger. A jet of liquid squirts out and splashes over the panel that activates the door.

After a moment, the panel begins to melt with a fizzing sound. The metal casing starts buckling and the panel itself begins to bubble and blister.

Then the whole lot explodes in a shower of sparks, sending all three of you jumping backwards.

The door slides open with a gentle sigh.

The Doctor and Martha look at you, dumbfounded.

'I don't know what's in that water pistol,' says the Doctor, 'but, please, be careful where you point it!'

You run into the Wet Dock. One of the Sea Bikes is missing — and so is Jolla.

It's time to uncover the secret of the abyss. Turn to 35.

3 The corridor bends to the left. You are so busy staring at the corridor's curved white walls that you walk smack into a tall man with a thick white beard and a wisp of white hair on his head.

He appears to be wearing an old navy uniform — a thick blue wool jacket with gold buttons and a white woollen pullover underneath. A gold badge on his chest says *Jacques*.

He rests a heavy hand on your shoulder. His face is ruddy and creased from a life spent outdoors. You have to look up because he is a good deal taller than you.

'Watch where you're going!' he says, in a firm, but not unkind, voice. 'You lot must be Lubbers. Well, you've lost your way to the welcoming speech. It's back that way in the Presentation Pod!'

To turn back to the Presentation Pod turn to 32. To press on around the corridor, turn to 5.

4 You need to get up to the Wet Dock — and quick! You scramble to find the nearest personal transportation vehicles.

The Doctor scoots up behind you on one of the little two-seater buggies. He slows down as he passes, so you can hop on-board.

The second you're sitting in the passenger seat, the Doctor puts his foot down and speeds off down the main corridor.

The sprinklers are still going full pelt and there's a couple of centimetres of water on the floor. The wheels of the cart are sending up a huge amount of spray.

Just when you think you couldn't possibly go any faster, Martha pulls up alongside you — and then overtakes you… with Marion in the passenger seat and Flux clinging on to the back!

You skid to a halt, tumble out of the buggies and race to the Wet Dock.

Go to 78.

5 You hang around for a minute and then, when you think no one's looking, all three of you stride quickly and purposefully down the corridor. It's pretty quiet, as everyone important is probably in the presentation.

The Doctor wonders out loud where on Earth — indeed when on Earth — you might be.

But you are not so concerned. You feel a bubble of laughter rise in your chest, as you enjoy the thrill of being in a completely unknown place and disobeying instructions! Martha joins in with your hilarity, linking up with you and leaning against you as you walk.

You stop dead in your tracks as a deep voice, loaded with menace, floats from a circular doorway.

'Hey! Who are you?' says the voice. 'And why aren't you in the presentation?'

You need to think quickly! To return to the presentation, turn to 32. If you want the Doctor to confront the person with the menacing voice, go to 34.

6 You're alone with Jacques in the Hub.

You remember that, when you first encountered him, you thought Jacques was a bit of a scary, angry old man. But now — slumped down in his chair — he just looks old.

He tells you that the Corinthian has been his life's work — and now the work of his son and his family in turn.

The entire future of the Project depends on tomorrow's presentation to the United World Council. And now it looks like Jolla's determined to sabotage the whole thing — but why?

You reassure Jacques that the Doctor is on the case — and promise him that you'll do your best to sort the whole thing out.

You look up to the monitors and you see that Jolla is in the Wet Dock. He's getting into a Sea Bike and heading down to the airlock.

Get over to the Wet Dock now and see if you can keep your promise to Jacques!

Turn to 35.

7 Scripps uses a personal communicator to call up someone called Flux. Scripps explains to you that Flux will take you to the Wet Dock, and show you some of the advances the Corinthian Project team have made in the area of vehicle engineering.

It all sounds pretty high level, so you are surprised to discover that Flux is a ten-year-old boy with curly ginger hair! He's quite a confident kid, and a bit of a know-it-all. And no wonder — it turns out that Scripps is Flux's Dad and that Flux has spent his whole life on-board the Project!

As you walk around the hoop-shaped structure in a clockwise direction from the East Quadrant, you pass many round doorways that lead off the main loop. You pass Recreation Pods, Accommodation Pods and a Canteen Pod before eventually reaching the Wet Dock.

Now check out the Sea Bikes! Go to 36.

8 The Doctor pilots the Mini Sub out to the edge of the abyss while you keep a sharp eye out for trouble. The sight of a mean-looking shark momentarily troubles you, but there's no sign of Jolla.

The Doctor turns to you and Martha and says, 'Are you ready for a close encounter?'

Before you can answer, the Doctor switches off the engines. The Sub drifts over the edge and sinks silently...

You see the rocky wall of the abyss slide past the window.

And then it goes dark. It's as though the whole craft has been slipped into a black velvet bag. The Doctor hits a switch. A bright light illuminates the exterior of the Sub.

You are surrounded by writhing, shadowy figures. Each one is about the size of an adult human and roughly the same shape — except for a fish-like tail instead of legs!

'You're kidding me!' says Martha. 'Mermaids?'

'They have been mistaken for mermaids in the past,' says the Doctor. 'But these are Dax — hmm, I thought they'd been wiped out when the Daleks destroyed Daxus.'

'Daxus?' says Martha.

'The water planet,' says the Doctor. 'Their home.'

A Dax floats up to the window. It appears to be looking at you — but you can't make out any eyes. The whole creature is covered in an opaque black membrane underneath which its muscles twitch and flutter. The Dax darts away — it's so quick you don't even see it flick its tail.

'What are they doing here?' asks Martha.

'It's a good question,' says the Doctor. 'Perhaps they're looking for a new home. They mean no harm. They're a benevolent race.'

And that's when a massive explosion rocks the Sub.

To grab the controls of the Sub, turn to 37. To call for help, turn to 42.

9 Flux lowers a Sea Bike into the Sea Dock. He's just showing you how to pilot it, when a shrill voice pipes, 'Hey! What do you think you're doing?'

It's a girl, the same height as Flux. She has the same smattering of freckles and the same colour hair — only hers is tied up in a high ponytail.

'Shut up, Sis!' says Flux. 'These guys are from the Ocean Futures Organisation. They know what they're doing!'

'I don't see why they need to go out in those things,' huffs the girl. 'They can see just as well from the viewing window.'

'That's my twin, Marion,' Flux whispers to you. 'She's a real goody-goody.'

'I heard that!' says Marion, pinching her brother's arm.

Martha volunteers to join Marion on the viewing platform.

To go out on a Sea Bike, turn to 16. To hang back and visit the viewing platform, turn to 17.

10 The roar of the bubbles fades away. You feel like you are drifting off to sleep.

Your Sea Bike is lifted from the yawning mouth of the abyss and back up to the coral reef.

You can see the Doctor's Sea Bike being pushed along by shadowy figures with flickering tails! You must be dreaming!

Your Sea Bike bounces gently on the ocean floor and the shadowy figures disappear as fast as jumping fleas.

The Doctor's Sea Bike nudges against yours and there's a gasping sound as your cab fills with fresh air.

The Doctor explains that the green switch activates the R.A.C. — not the blue switch. What was Jolla thinking?

You ask the Doctor how you made it out of the abyss. 'Good question!' he says. 'And we're not leaving the Project until we find out the answer.'

You limp back into the Wet Dock, sharing the Doctor's oxygen supply.

Turn to 20.

11 | **A**s the Doctor's bike drifts away, it begins to pick up speed, swept along by a deep-sea current.

'I'm drifting towards the abyss,' says the Doctor, firmly and clearly through your headphones. 'Line up beside me, and push me into that coral harbour!'

You twist the accelerator hard and race over to the Doctor's side. You try to hold your speeding vehicle steady as you line up against the Doctor's Sea Bike. But the left wing of your vehicle clips the right wing of the Doctor's Sea Bike, sending it spinning wildly out of control.

The Doctor says something about trying to activate the Sea Bike's navigation system and gyroscope. But his voice breaks up in your headphones.

It still might not be too late to call for help, and turn to 13. Or hope for the best, turn to 38.

12 You pull out the water pistol, filled with whatever it was that melted the control panel outside the Wet Dock. Maybe some kind of chemical fertiliser? Whatever it was, you guess it's strong enough to melt the internal wall of the Sub.

It's a crazy idea but you've got to do something. After all, someone's letting off explosions while you and your companions are trapped in a leaky Sub, under a landslide, at the bottom of the ocean... surrounded by weird aliens.

This whole thing couldn't get any crazier.

You fumble around the sides of the Sub, trying to locate the leak. You take a deep breath... and fire the water pistol at the wall of the Sub.

'What are you doing?' cries Martha, as the lining wall of the Sub begins to bubble and melt. 'Are you crazy?'

But the internal wall melts over the leaking crack, sealing you in. Good going!

Turn to 43.

13 You punch the red emergency button in the centre of the Sea Bike's handlebar controls and a new voice comes over your headphones. It's not Flux, Scripps or even Flux's Grandpa Jacques — but a man calling himself Jolla.

He seems unconcerned that the Doctor is racing towards the abyss and speaks calmly and steadily through your headphones.

He instructs you to drive close to the Doctor's Sea Bike and activate the Rescue Aid Connection by flipping the blue switch in the panel set into the glass above your head.

The Doctor's Sea Bike is spinning wildly. You drive as close as you dare. You are about to flip the blue switch when Flux shouts over your headphones, 'Don't hit that switch!'

Do you follow Jolla's instructions and flip the blue switch? Turn to 19. Or pay attention to Flux and ignore Jolla? Turn to 15.

14 'He's going down into the abyss!' yells Martha, slapping the glass window with the palms of her hands.

You are about to start yelling for help when Martha grabs your arm.

'Hey,' she cries. 'Wait a minute! He's coming back up!'

Sure enough, the Doctor's Sea Bike appears to be rising out of the abyss... It looks as though it is being lifted by... Well, it's hard to see, but they look like shadows.

Perhaps they're manatees or sea cows. You're not sure what a sea cow is or what one looks like but you know that ancient mariners supposedly mistook them for mermaids.

The Doctor's Sea Bike settles down in a sort of harbour in the coral. The shadowy shapes around his Sea Bike flicker and disappear, as though they were never there.

You race down to the Wet Dock to catch up with the Doctor.

Turn to 20.

15 Flux is shouting something through your headphones about the blue switch expelling oxygen but in your panic you can't make it out.

The man calling himself Jolla instructs you once again to flip the blue switch and activate the Rescue Aid Connection.

The Doctor's voice crackles over your headphones in a burst of static. 'I'm not sure about this,' he shouts.

'I maintain these vehicles myself,' says Jolla, his voice as calm and flat as a lake on a still day. 'I know what I'm talking about.'

You glance at the blue switch, and the green switch next to it. As you look up, your Sea Bike glances off the rocky edge of the abyss, knocking the controls right out of your hands.

You're swerving all over the place. Your Sea Bike collides with the Doctor's Sea Bike with a sickening crack. The water around you seems to explode, churning with bubbles.

Turn to 10.

You are left struggling with the controls of your Sea Bike while the Doctor speeds out of the airlock and across the seabed, away from the Corinthian Project.

To accelerate, you have to turn the right hand grip of the handlebars towards you. To slow down, you have to turn the left hand grip away from you. It takes you a while to get the hang of this — and to remember to steer at the same time!

The Doctor's voice comes through your headphones. It's as clear as if he were alongside you. He tells you that he's used this kind of transport before, for exploration in a helium rich atmosphere. The controls are identical. You twist the accelerator and speed over to where the Doctor waits for you to catch up.

It's not until you stop and take a moment to look back that you realise the true wonder of the Corinthian Project. It's a white, hoop-shaped structure, divided into four sections — like a giant life belt that has been anchored to the ocean floor.

On the north side of the Project, the ground slopes away towards what you guess might be the abyss that Flux mentioned. On the south side, hundreds of clear domes are organised in a grid, stretching as far away as you can see. Near to you, to the north west side of the Project, is the stunning coral reef that Flux took a chunk out of. But strangest of all, rising up from the circle at the centre of the structure, is the rusting hulk of a sunken cruise liner.

You're about to say something to the Doctor about this amazing sight, when you realise he's drifted away from you. He explains, over your headphones, that his Sea Bike has cut out and he can't get it restarted.

Do you attempt to rescue the Doctor and his drifting bike? Go to11. Or call for help and risk the wrath of Flux's Grandpa Jacques? Go to13.

17 | The Doctor climbs on-board a Sea Bike. The bubble of the cab closes around him and seals itself with a hiss. You leave the Dock, just as Flux launches the Doctor's Sea Bike down a ramp, where it slides into an airlock. You walk up to the viewing platform and join Martha and Marion. You stand by a large, circular window and look out across the seabed. The view is pretty awesome. The seascape is so unfamiliar to you that it almost looks like an alien planet.

You see the Doctor speeding along on a Sea Bike.

'That looks pretty precarious,' says Martha.

'Oh, Sea Bikes are perfectly safe,' says Marion. 'Providing you know how to use them.'

The Doctor seems to know what he's doing, but you're glad you didn't go out there. He scoots over to the coral reef that Flux pranged. The colours are impossibly bright — hot pink, deep red, vibrant orange and sunny yellow. It doesn't look real. After that, the ground slopes away to what you guess must be the edge of the abyss that Flux mentioned. The thought of what might be down there makes you shiver.

'Hey!' shouts Martha, making you jump. 'What's happening to the Doctor?'

You see the Doctor's Sea Bike is spinning out of control and heading towards the abyss.

'I've never seen that happen before,' says Marion. 'What's the matter with his Bike?'

'How do we know?' says Martha. 'We just have to get the Doctor back to safety!'

'We'd better call Jolla,' says Marion. 'He'll know what to do.'

If you want to do as Marion says and call for help, go to 14. If you want to grab the other Sea Bike and go out and help the Doctor, turn to page 21.

18 The inside of the Decontamination Zone looks like nothing more than a hi-tech car wash — for humans.

An automated voice explains to you that you are about to, 'Undergo a series of procedures designed to protect the environment, the Project and the individual.'

The machine subjects you to a radiated cleansing shower and various tests. Flux, Marion, Martha and yourself pass through the procedure without difficulty but the machine struggles to process the Doctor's data.

Martha talks about the dark shapes she thought she saw coming out of the abyss and you wonder why the Sea Bikes had not been left in a good state of repair — isn't that supposed to be the Chief Engineer's job?

All agree that further investigation is necessary — which is handy because the Doctor is using the sonic screwdriver to open a hatch in the ceiling!

Do you wait and see if Jacques turns up to take you to his Pod, as instructed? Turn to 22. Or sneak out through the ceiling hatch? Turn to 75.

19 | Struggling to keep control of your Sea Bike with one hand, you reach up to the control panel above your head and flip the blue switch.

You wait a second for the Rescue Aid Connection to kick in. You're not exactly sure what it's going to do. There's a huge roar and the water around you churns with bubbles. Your Sea Bike bounces like an ice cube in a fizzy drink. This can't be right!

You are now hurtling uncontrollably towards the abyss. And, as if that wasn't bad enough, a needle flickers on a dial in front of you informing you that the oxygen level inside your vehicle is plummeting.

You feel faint. Your heartbeat thumps in your ears as you struggle to breathe. Bubbles churn fiercely in the water all around you. You don't even know which way is up any more.

Turn to 10.

Flux is waiting for you in the Wet Dock — along with a man in a buttoned-up, spotless white lab coat with a stern face below neatly parted blonde hair.

'He looks angry,' you whisper to Flux.

'That's Jolla — he always looks like that,' says Flux. 'But, right now, he really is angry.'

'Everyone who ventures out of the Project has to be automatically decontaminated,' says Jolla. Despite his bad temper, his voice is flat and emotionless.

Martha protests that not all of you left the building, but Jolla is insistent that you must all undergo the decontamination process. 'Partly for security,' he says, 'and partly as punishment for leaving the Project without permission.'

'But that's not fair,' says Martha. She turns to the Doctor for support, but he is busy examining a Sea Bike with his sonic screwdriver.

Jolla exits. You all turn to the Doctor to see what he has to say but he is engrossed. He tinkers with the controls of the Sea Bike.

Marion explains that Jolla is the Chief Engineer of the Project. 'He's not very well liked but he's the second in command

and he's always organised and reliable,' she says. 'We'd better do as he says.'

This last comment finally gets the Doctor's attention.

'There's something fishy about Jolla,' he says. 'He maintains that these vehicles were in good working order, when they clearly weren't. I might not be standing here now if it wasn't for the...'

The Doctor is interrupted as Flux and Marion's grandpa Jacques storms into the Wet Dock. He looks agitated and his white beard is all a twitch as he orders you all to wait for him in the Decontamination Zone and he will take you to his Pod.

Turn to 18.

21 You dash down to the Wet Dock and tell Flux that the Doctor's in trouble and you have to take the other Sea Bike out there and help him.

'What's the problem?' asks Flux.

As you jump into the other Sea Bike, you tell him that the Doctor's Sea Bike is out of control and he is heading towards the abyss.

'That's impossible,' says Flux. 'Jolla checks the Sea Bikes all the time, and makes sure they're always in good working order.'

There's no time to ask who this 'Jolla' is. You just need to know how to get the Sea Bike started! Flux races through an explanation of how to use the controls, and launches you down to the airlock.

The last thing you see before the water swallows you up is Flux waving at you to put on your headphones so you can keep in touch.

Turn to page 38.

22 | Jacques arrives and takes you to his Pod. It's just like an old-fashioned office or a headmaster's study with a heavy wooden desk and lots of books.

He tells you that he does not want you to leave the Project — except in larger craft crewed by his trusted staff. He says that if you go against his wishes you will lose your right to be honoured guests, and you may be confined to a secure Pod.

He explains that he fears not only for your safety but also for the entire Project — it is in great danger.

Martha asks him about the dark shapes she saw rising from the abyss. What were they? Are they dangerous?

He brushes off the question and advises you to stay out of trouble. Clearly rattled, Jacques hurries out of his Pod.

The Doctor observes that Jacques seems to be hiding something.

Turn to 24 to sneakily follow Jacques or turn to 49 to search his Pod.

23 There's not much any of you can do against Jolla when he's piloting a Sea Bike and you're not.

He revs up the Bike and races away towards the Bio Dome fields.

You swim after him, kicking out as hard as you can, but there's no way you're going to catch him.

You're suddenly aware of a very strange sensation. It feels like there's an ice cube melting inside your head. And you can hear a voice... Or rather... Voices.

'We are the Dax,' whisper the voices. 'We're so far away from home...'

A dark shadow rises up above you. It looks like a giant sea creature. But it isn't — it's a swarm of aliens, the Dax — moving as one.

They cluster over the Bio Domes and a series of muffled explosions scatter stunned Dax across the ocean floor! And you suddenly feel terribly sad.

You wonder why the Dax would want to blow up the Bio Domes. Which is when you get the strange sensation again and the voices say, 'No more explodings.'

Then you understand that they're containing the explosions, not making them.

The Dax gather around Jolla's Sea Bike, holding it against the ocean floor.

There's one more muffled explosion, and a ripple passes through the swarming Dax.

Flux is waving at you. He points towards the Project and beckons you, urgently.

You start to feel dizzy.

Perhaps the liquid from the sachet is wearing off.

You're blacking out... And the last thing you see before you pass out... Is Jolla, swimming away from the wreck of his Sea Bike. He must have had one of those sachets — just like you. And you wonder how far he can swim before he passes out... Just... like... you...

Turn to 50.

24 Tailing Jacques without being spotted is tricky. You're concentrating so hard that you suddenly realise you've lost contact with the others.

By looking at the signs above the doors, you work out you're in the West Quadrant — the Study Quarter. The nearest Pod to you is labelled the Corinthian Archive — and that's where Jacques is heading.

You creep into the Archive Pod, right behind Jacques.

Jacques is rifling through some cabinets and pulling out handfuls of small plastic cards. He starts snapping the cards in two. You suspect they contain information that he doesn't want anyone to see.

The Doctor appears. He must have made it to the Archive before you! He snatches one of the cards away from Jacques and demands to know why he is destroying the archive.

Jacques sighs and says, 'It's the abyss.' But rather than explain further, he says 'It's easier if I show you.'

Go to the Hub. Turn to 28.

You shrug and say you don't know anything about it.

Scripps says to Jolla, 'Why don't you search the memory card? If anyone has been out to the wreck, you'll soon see.'

Jolla starts scrolling through the footage from the camera fixed on the wreck. You share an anxious look with the Doctor and Martha. Martha jerks a thumb in the direction of a doorway and the three of you sneak out.

You hurry past the Wet Dock and duck into the nearest Pod — aware that Jolla could be watching you from the Hub.

A shaft of light from the corridor splashes across the floor of a gloomy, circular living space.

'Lights,' says Martha. Nothing happens.

'I don't know about this voice activation malarkey,' she says. 'What was wrong with switches?'

As you look around, you realise you're in Jolla's Pod — his personal living space.

That's lucky! Or is it…?

To stay and explore, turn to 76. To exit, turn to 79.

26 | The camera tilts down over the edge of the abyss and the whole screen turns to black. The camera struggles to find something on which to focus in the seemingly bottomless abyss...

Someone behind the camera hits a light and it bounces back off the blackness. That's when you realise — you all realise — that the blackness is moving! It's a seething mass of something... Lots of things... Undulating and flexing and rolling over the top of each other.

You can't make out any individual shapes but whatever's in the abyss, there's loads of them and they're most definitely alive!

Suddenly, like a scene from a scary movie, something shoots towards the camera and makes you jump.

It looked like a dark, shadowy... mermaid!

Jolla slams the eject button on the side of the monitor and the memory card pops out. He catches it and runs out of the Hub. The Doctor and Martha chase after him.

To chase after Jolla, turn to 30. To stay with Jacques, turn to 6.

27 You crawl to the right and find another ceiling hatch. The Doctor unlocks it and slides it open. You peek down to the corridor below. There doesn't seem to be anyone around so you give the Doctor the thumbs up.

The Doctor lowers himself down and helps you and Martha down into the corridor.

'Look out,' says Martha. 'Here comes Jacques!'

You duck into a doorway and hold your breath.

You see Jacques stop underneath the ceiling hatch. You didn't replace it properly after you jumped down. You hope he doesn't notice it...

But he does! He looks up, quizzically at the open hatch. He looks around and you duck back behind the doorway, hoping he hasn't seen you.

You hear him press some sort of intercom and report the open hatch to the Services Department. And then you hear him walking away with fast, purposeful strides.

'Quick,' says the Doctor. 'Let's follow him!'

Turn to 24.

The Hub is situated in the North Quadrant — the Service Quarter of the Corinthian Project. It is not at the centre of the building, but you can see now that it is the centre of operations.

Banks of TV screens relay images from cameras around the entire Project. You are entranced by the flickering monitors — each one a window into someone's busy life.

You see scientists hard at work in the Science and Study Quarters and people chilling out in the Social Quarter. You can even see Flux and Marion in the Storage Pod where you started your journey. They're looking at the TARDIS with some curiosity!

You see the Wet Dock where a Sea Bike is draining on the dry rack after a spin out to the abyss. You see the wreck of the old Corinthian at the centre of the Project. And a view of the Canteen Pod reminds you that you haven't eaten properly for ages...

Jolla bursts in, brandishing what looks like a water pistol. He waves it in Jacques' direction — and this reminds you of why you have come here! To find out what it is that Jacques has seen — and why Jolla wants to find out about it!

Jolla looks directly at you. His eyes are cold and hard, his voice expressionless. He says, 'You have no right to be in the Hub. You're a threat to security.'

'You have no right to withhold your observations from the Ocean Futures Organisation,' says the Doctor, stepping in between you and Jolla.

'That's what I came here to show you,' says Jacques. And he inserts a memory card into a slot alongside one of the monitors.

You all watch in silence as the monitor shows a recording of a journey into the abyss...

Turn to 26.

'What is it you want?' says Jacques, his voice floating up through a cooling vent.

The Doctor gives you the thumbs up — you chose the right way through the ceiling space!

You're above an Archive Pod — and Jacques is down below. But who is he talking to?

'You know the secret of the abyss,' says a voice. You recognise the flat, monotone drawl. It's Jolla — the Chief Engineer!

'I have no idea what you mean,' says Jacques.

'You believe the Corinthian Project is in great danger,' says Jolla.

'What on Earth makes you think that?' says Jacques.

'I was watching you from the Hub and I heard you talking to those strangers from the O.F.O.,' says Jolla. 'I warn you, I have plans for my work here that exceed anything you can imagine. I must have the evidence.'

'I have suspected that you were less than completely loyal for some time,' says Jacques. 'And you can put away that weapon — it will be useless against the danger we face in the darker regions of the abyss.'

You exchange a look with Martha. Jolla's armed! The Doctor tries to get a better look through the cooling vent but none of you can see Jolla.

'Here — take these memory cards to your office,' Jacques continues. 'You can see for yourself what's down there.'

'Very well,' says Jolla. 'But I warn you not to mess about with me. I'll keep this weapon to hand.'

Jolla and Jacques exit from the room below. The Doctor unlocks the cooling vent and slides it to one side. He lowers himself down and then helps you and Martha down.

You wonder what Jacques meant by 'your office'?

'He must mean the Hub — Jolla's domain,' says the Doctor.

'Quick!' says Martha. 'To the Hub!'

Turn to page 28.

30 You overtake the Doctor and Martha who seem to be distracted by something near the entrance to the Hub.

You run flat out after Jolla — but he jumps on-board a small vehicle that looks like a golf buggy. He speeds off. As fast as you can run you're never going to catch him.

You stop and lean against the wall, holding your side where you can feel the beginning of a stitch.

You hear an electric whining sound. It grows louder. You look around.

It's the Doctor — on another one of those electric buggies! And he's about to hit you!

The vehicle squeals to a halt nearly throwing Martha out of the front passenger seat. It stops so close, you can feel the front bumper against your knee.

'Come on!' yells Martha.

But there are only two seats in the buggy.

Do you jump on the back of the buggy? Turn to 61. Or walk back to the Hub? Turn to 6.

31 After returning to the Dock, you meet up with everyone else in the Canteen Pod. Scripps is in a hurry to talk to Chief Engineer Jolla.

The Doctor expresses an interest in finding out about the canister mysteriously stuck to the side of the Bio Dome. Scripps asks you to come to the Hub later on and he will tell you what he's found out about it.

Meanwhile he leaves you with the two people he feels are most qualified to tell you all about life on-board the Corinthian Project... his two kids — Flux and Marion!

Marion is obviously Flux's twin sister. She is the same age and has the same kind of unruly ginger hair, only tied up in a bouncy ponytail.

She has a similar smattering of freckles across an open, cheeky-looking face. She's even wearing the same kind of navy blue boiler suit.

To get something to eat, turn to 39. If you just want to grab a drink, turn to 63.

The sound of chatter echoes down the corridor, which bends off to the right. The Doctor observes that, wherever you are, it must be some sort of circular structure.

Various smartly dressed people, holding drinks, mill around a sign: The Corinthian Project welcomes the U.W.C.

A middle-aged man with a black beard stands in front of a round doorway. You spot the words 'Presentation Pod' in curved letters around the top.

The man grins at you and your companions while glancing at your chest. 'No name badges?' he says. 'Never mind! I'm Scripps!'

He shakes your hand firmly and thrusts a sheet of paper into your other hand, saying, 'Welcome to the Project!' He slaps your back, heartily, almost shoving you through the doorway into a vast, glass dome.

All three of you stop dead — because you can now see that you are on the bottom of the ocean.

Scripps barges past. 'Grab a seat,' he says. 'The welcome speech is about to begin!'

To look at the sheet of paper, turn to 96.
To hear the speech, turn to 85. Or tiptoe
back out, turn to 5.

33 You run inside the Wet Dock, just in time to see Jolla sliding down the ramp on a Sea Bike.

He smiles at you as he sinks into the airlock. It's the first time you've seen him smile. It's not a nice smile — in fact, it's the opposite of nice.

It takes a minute for the airlock to operate a full cycle. The Doctor tries to deactivate it, to trap Jolla inside.

You run up to the viewing platform, where you see the Doctor is too late. Jolla is speeding away on his Sea Bike.

'Looks like we're going out,' says the Doctor.

'But what about those things we saw?' says Martha. 'On the monitor.'

'Forget about those,' says the Doctor. 'It's Jolla we've got to worry about.'

Turn to 35.

34 'I could ask you the same questions,' says the Doctor, stepping up to the doorway... Only to be confronted by... A boy, aged about ten, with curly ginger hair. He slips a voice-changing chip into the breast pocket of his overalls and laughs.

'My name's Flux. I've lived in the Project my whole life. So, I don't need to see a stupid presentation about it,' the boy shrugs. 'But I've never seen you lot around here.'

You introduce yourself and the Doctor and Martha do likewise.

'If you know so much,' says the Doctor, 'why don't you show us around?'

'Well, I was on my way to the Wet Dock,' says Flux. 'If you want to see the Bio Domes, you'd better find my Dad — look out for a man called Scripps.'

Turn to 54 to find Scripps and see what goes on in the mysterious Bio Domes. If you want to check out the Wet Dock with Flux, go to 36.

35 None of you really fancy going after Jolla on the remaining Sea Bike.

The Doctor, using the sonic screwdriver, starts unlocking a series of garage doors. One by one, the doors slide upwards and you see what's behind them — various underwater vehicles in different states of repair.

While the Doctor works, you and Martha try and get everything straight in your heads.

'So, tomorrow is the big presentation to the U.W.C.' says Martha.

You remember that Jacques was trying to destroy all the evidence of his trips.

'He's trying to stop us from finding out about something,' says Martha. 'And, whatever it is, Jolla doesn't like it either.'

You wonder just exactly what it could be.

'I think I know the answer,' says the Doctor as the final garage door rises to reveal a cool-looking four-seater submarine.

Do you jump on-board the Mini Sub with the Doctor and Martha? Turn to 8. Or opt to stay behind. Turn to 44.

36 Flux explains that the Wet Dock is the Pod where undersea vehicles are maintained and dispatched. And the best way to get an overall view of the Project — and the coral reef and the abyss nearby — is by using Sea Bikes — cool-looking, single pilot transportation in which you can zip around underwater.

Flux shows you some Sea Bikes up on the dry rack. They look a bit like jet skis, only contained in a clear bubble, so you can ride them underwater without a diving suit.

Flux says that his grandpa — Jacques — has put an embargo on him using the Sea Bikes. This is because Flux pranged one on the reef, damaging some coral that was hundreds of years old!

The Doctor says, 'But how can we get a good view of the Project without leaving the building?'

Flux says, 'Hey, just because I can't use a Sea Bike, doesn't mean you shouldn't take a spin out!'

Want to take a trip on a Sea Bike? Go to 9.
Or go and find Scripps again? Turn to 54.

37 The force of the explosion knocks you all out of your seats. You grab the controls, and try to steer the Sub out of trouble while the Doctor attempts to contact Jacques back at the Project.

There is chaos all around you as the Dax swim around in a panic. A second explosion blows away the rock on one side of the abyss.

You try to restart the engine, but instead you just switch off the exterior lights plunging everything into darkness as a landslide engulfs the Sub.

After a terrifying moment, the emergency lights come on inside the Sub — bathing all three of you in an eerie green light.

'What's this?' says Martha.

'A landslide,' says the Doctor. 'We're trapped.'

'No,' says Martha. 'This!'

Her feet are wet. There's a leak in the Sub.

Did you pick up Jolla's weapon outside the Wet Dock? Turn to 12. If not, turn to 62.

38 | As you accelerate towards the Doctor, you realise you are approaching the edge of the abyss. The ocean bed begins to slope away from beneath you and you can see the chasm yawning ahead.

You twist the left grip of your Sea Bike. The brakes whine, but the Sea Bike does not slow down. Now both of you are being pulled down into the blackness of the abyss.

Suddenly a great surge of water seems to emanate from deep below, lifting you out of danger. The shock of the surge is so strong that it knocks you out of the seat of your Sea Bike.

For a moment, you are stunned. A moment later, you realise that both you and the Doctor have drifted into the shelter of the coral harbour.

Now you must tow the Doctor back to the Wet Dock and everyone will have to face the music.

Turn to 20.

39 Marion shows you around the kitchens in the back of the Canteen Pod. It is all brushed steel and glass, and illuminated by bright white lights.

You don't see any implements you recognise like a kettle or a grill. Not even a saucepan. You think it looks more like a laboratory than a kitchen.

Marion offers you a tray of assorted 'tasters' — so you can experience Corinthian cuisine.

You try a couple of mouthfuls of different things. It is all delicious.

That's when Marion explains that most of the food is made from different strains of seaweed. The rest is made from shellfish.

'Bleurgh!' says Martha. 'I'm glad you didn't tell me that before I tried the 'chicken'... Otherwise I might never have tried it. But, actually — it was really quite nice!'

'Now you've tried some seaweed,' says Marion, 'I dare you to take up a real challenge!'

Turn to 66 to find out what it is.

40 | The Doctor says, 'Cheers!' And all three of you rip off the top of your sachets and suck out the contents.

Your mouth fills with a thick, metallic-tasting liquid. It's so foul, you almost spit it right out. But you force yourself to swallow it.

You take one last gulp of air as the Sub fills with seawater. But the air makes your lungs burn and you start to cough! What was in those sachets? Poison?

The water subsumes you. You have no air left in your lungs. There's nothing you can do except gulp seawater...and discover that you can breathe underwater!

You look around at Martha and the Doctor. They are both grinning. The Doctor gives you a big thumbs up.

But there's no time to enjoy this new sensation.

The Sub is collapsing like a juice carton. A hole bursts open in the side of the Sub and all three of you swim outside into the open sea.

And not a second too late! The south wall of the abyss is subsiding, and the Sub slips down and is swallowed by the black water below.

You wonder what's happened to the Dax? You guess they were frightened away by the explosions.

You're gazing down into the blackness below when you feel a tap on your shoulder. You look around — it's Flux! He's obviously used a sachet as well, because he's swimming around without any diving gear.

He is wearing headphones and a face mike but, now that your intercom's gone down with the Sub, these are useless.

Flux taps his wrist and winds his index fingers around each other. You guess this means that you haven't got long before whatever was in those sachets wears off.

All four of you swim up to the mouth of the abyss — and come face to face with Jolla on his Sea Bike.

Turn to 23.

41 The Doctor rips off the top of a sachet. Martha does the same.

The Doctor says, 'Cheers!' and the Doctor and Martha swallow the contents of the sachet. You take one last gulp of air as the Sub fills with seawater. You let the sachet slip from your fingers.

The Sub is collapsing like a juice carton, but the water dulls the sound of twisting metal. A hole bursts open in the side of the Sub and all three of you swim outside into the open sea.

You're barely a metre away from the Sub when the wall of the abyss subsides further and a whole lot of rocks come sliding down, sending the twisted remains of the Sub down into the murky blackness.

Your lungs are already starting to burn from holding your breath and your chest feels like it's being crushed by the weight of the sea.

You're blacking out… and the last thing you see before you pass out… is the Doctor and Martha… looking at each other… and laughing!

Turn to 50.

42 You're relieved to hear Jacques' voice crackling over the intercom. He explains about the explosion.

'It's Jolla,' he says. 'I think he's using the explosives that were used to level the seabed during the building of the Bio Dome fields.'

'He's obviously gunning to get rid of us — and the Dax,' says the Doctor as he struggles to regain control of the Sub. 'But he doesn't realise what he's doing. Look at the rock here. It's subsiding. Without the Dax, the south wall of the abyss would have collapsed by now — and taken the Project, all the research and everyone inside, along with it. A catastrophe!'

'And if the abyss caved in, the underwater landslide could cause a tsunami on the surface,' says Jacques.

As the Doctor starts up the Sub's motors and powers you out of the abyss, you think this couldn't possibly get any worse.

That's when you come face to face with Jolla.

Turn to 48.

43 The water's ankle deep in the bottom of the Sub — but at least no more is coming in.

'The Sub's propellors are trapped,' says the Doctor, taking back the controls. He restarts the motor, but there's not enough power to get you out from the under the rocks.

Martha leaps out of her seat and starts jumping around in the back of the Sub. Has she gone mad?

But your question is answered as the Sub suddenly tilts backwards.

'That's it!' says the Doctor, revving up the engines. 'Keep going!'

You and Martha jump up and down in the back of the Sub, laughing as you splash about.

There's a stomach churning scrape — followed by a sound like soot sliding down a chimney, only a hundred times as loud — and the Sub breaks free from the landslide!

You power out of the abyss and come face to face with Jolla.

Turn to 48.

44 | Before sealing up the Mini Sub, the Doctor tosses you a pair of headphones and urges you to keep in touch.

You rush up to the viewing platform. There's no sign of Jolla but, after a minute, you spot the Mini Sub heading out to the abyss.

As cheeky as young Flux and his twin sister Marion were, you kind of wish they were around right now. You feel pretty alone up there on the viewing platform. Still — you've got to hold it together for the Doctor and Martha.

The Doctor turns off the engines. The Sub begins to drift down into the abyss.

As the Doctor and Martha disappear into the abyss, another vessel appears. It's Jolla on the Sea Bike!

Do you try to call out to the Doctor using your mike? Turn to 65. Or go and grab the remaining Sea Bike? Race to 46.

45 'So what are they, then?' asks Martha. 'Little packets of seaweed? What's that going to do?'

'You take one of these,' says Flux, 'And you can breathe underwater!'

Martha laughs. You look at her. 'You're joking, Flux,' she says. 'Aren't you?'

'No,' says Flux. 'These are for real, I swear!'

'It's true!' says Marion. 'They're still in development, so don't tell Dad we took them — but we've tried them out, haven't we Flux?'

'Yeah, but only in the swimming pool, not in the sea,' says Flux. He quickly adds, 'They work though! Don't they, Marion?'

'The effect lasts about ten minutes,' says Marion. 'It's a weird sensation.'

You look at the Doctor — perhaps he has seen such a thing before on his travels. He just smiles at you and shrugs. It's your call.

If you still want to try the sachets, turn bravely to 69. If you'd rather use the more familiar-looking scuba-diving gear, go to 64.

46 You slide the Sea Bike down to the airlock and climb inside. You hope you can remember what Flux told you about the controls.

To accelerate, you have to turn the right hand grip of the handlebars towards you. To slow down, you have to turn the left hand grip away from you...

You're about to activate the airlock when there's a banging on the side of the Bike. You're annoyed to be interrupted at this crucial moment — the Doctor's in trouble and he needs your help!

It's Flux. He's wearing a face mike, but you can't hear him. You take off your headphones, pop the seal on the Sea Bike and slide open the canopy. You ask Flux what he wants.

'Jolla's been tampering with the Bikes,' he says. 'So you don't want to go out on that Bike. Try this instead.' Flux hands you a sachet of liquid.

You ask him what it does.

Flux grins. 'You'll see!'

Turn to 59.

You all go through the airlock and step out onto the seabed.

Scripps leads you towards a shellfish Bio Dome. The inside of the glass hemisphere is crusted with grey and black shellfish.

Pipes and cables feed in and out of the Dome, monitoring everything including temperature, water quality and any by-products of the growing process such as minerals and gases.

You ask why you can't go inside the Domes.

'Inside each Dome is a carefully controlled mini ecosystem,' Scripps explains over the intercom. 'They are being constantly monitored. Any contamination could invalidate months — even years — worth of data.'

'Hey,' says Martha, 'what's that?'

She's spotted a crack in the Dome. It appears to have been made by a metal canister clinging, limpet-like, to the exterior of the Dome. Scripps is naturally very concerned.

'We'd better hurry back,' he says.

To head back to the Project, turn to 31.
To wander off with the Doctor, turn to 60.

You're in the Mini Sub and it's bigger than Jolla's Sea Bike. But he is armed, and you're not.

Instead of launching any more explosives, Jolla turns to get away. The Doctor revs up the Sub and speeds towards Jolla's Sea Bike.

The Doctor flicks on the communicator and tries to coax Jolla back into the Project. You're not sure if Jolla can even hear the Doctor, but the Sea Bike is faster than the Mini Sub, and Jolla races away in an easterly direction over to the Bio Dome fields.

Which is when you find out where the Dax have gone. They are swarming over the Bio Domes. A series of muffled explosions scatters Dax across the ocean floor. Some of them fall away, stunned, and lie motionless in the water before being helped back to the abyss by other Dax.

'Why are the Dax blowing up the Bio Domes?' Martha asks.

'They're not,' says the Doctor. 'They're merely trying to contain the explosions, planted there by Jolla.'

You wonder how the Dax knew about the explosives. The Doctor explains that they are psychic and so sensitive to disruptions in their surrounding environment. This is how they know about the explosives, and why they are acting together to save the Project from extensive damage.

Sharing a consciousness, the Dax act as one. Like a school of fish, or birds flocking in the sky, the enigmatic aliens swarm around Jolla's Sea Bike, engulfing it like a smoky cloud and pushing it down to the ocean floor.

There's one more muffled explosion, and a ripple passes through the swarming Dax.

Once again, the stunned Dax are rapidly rounded up and carried away down the abyss.

The Doctor pilots the Sub over to the wreckage of Jolla's Sea Bike. There's not much of it left.

'Selfless creatures, the Dax,' says the Doctor. 'They have endangered themselves to save us — and the Project.'

'But what's happened to Jolla?' asks Martha.

The Doctor shrugs.

You're not sure if he saw it too, but you're pretty sure you saw him being swept away — towards the abyss.

Turn to 51.

49 Marion doesn't like the idea of searching through her Grandfather's things. She says she's going to the Recreation Pod to watch TV. The Doctor encourages Flux to follow her.

That leaves you, Martha and the Doctor to have a good snoop around!

'If you had a secret document,' Martha wants to know, 'where would you keep it?'

'On Saturn,' suggests the Doctor. 'No one ever goes there.'

You mention a friend of yours who hides his diary behind a wardrobe.

'Of course!' says the Doctor. 'We need to look behind this filing cabinet — not in it!'

You move some seashells from the top of the cabinet and heave it a few inches to one side. Behind the cabinet there's nothing but clumps of dust.

'They should sack the cleaner,' observes Martha.

You step backwards. One of the seashells crunches under your foot. Ooops!

But in the smashed remains is some sort of memory card! It must have been hidden inside the shell!

'Nice work!' says the Doctor. He pops open Jacques' laptop and presses the card into a slot.

A couple of taps on the touch pad and the Doctor accesses the memory card. It appears to contain a series of films — each one a journey into the abyss!

You're about to see what Jacques has been looking at down the abyss when a message flashes up, 'Low battery. Unable to continue operation.'

'We're in a futuristic, experimental community on the seabed,' laughs Martha, 'but they haven't sorted out that old problem yet.'

'Oh, it's years yet until the human race perfects self-replicating energy cells,' says the Doctor. He ejects the memory card and holds it up. 'Now let's go to the Hub where all the data is collated and see if we can get to the bottom of this.'

Turn to 28.

You open your eyes. You're in bed and everything around you is white and sterile. You must be in the Medical Pod.

As you breathe in, your throat burns a little and your chest aches. You guess you must have swallowed some seawater.

'Hey, stranger!' says a voice. You turn over. It's Martha, sitting by your bed.

You smile. She ruffles your hair and says she'll send for a nurse. You mention that you thought she was a trainee Doctor. 'That's right,' she says. 'But I haven't done my medicines of the future module, yet!'

You push yourself up on your elbows and demand to know everything that has happened since you blacked out in the ocean.

Martha smiles and says, 'OK. But I'm only going to give you the short version, and then I'm going to call for the nurse.'

Martha tells you that Jacques and Scripps came along in a pair of awesome-looking Atmospheric Construction Suits used for maintaining the Project. They brought you to the Medical Pod and you've been here ever since.

Martha explains that Jolla had discovered that the Project was built over an oil bed. He was planning on discrediting all of Scripps' research and getting the Project shut down.

Then he could sell the results of his own experiments for personal profit, and sell the information about the oil bed to the highest bidder.

He didn't count on there being aliens in the abyss, mind you.

You ask after Flux and Marion — and the Doctor of course.

Martha tells you that Flux and Marion are safe and, as for the Doctor... Well, he's about to do a presentation to the United World Council!

A Nurse enters your room. Despite feeling a little woozy, you insist to her that you are fine — so that you can go and see the Doctor speak to the U.W.C.

Martha says she'll keep an eye on you and the Nurse reluctantly lets you go.

Turn to 57.

51 | Martha, Flux, Marion and yourself are back in the Canteen Pod, on-board the Corinthian Project. It's nothing like where you live but, right now, it feels like home.

You tuck into your burger and chips and wash each mouthful down with a swallow of seaweed shake. You say that you are absolutely ravenous.

'It must be the sea air,' jokes Martha. 'It's given you an appetite,'

Scripps and Jacques enter, all smiles. Jacques offers you his hand and you have to wipe off the seaweed relish before you can shake it. Scripps claps you heartily on the back.

Scripps pulls up a chair and explains to you all that is now known about Jolla.

It turns out that he had discovered that the Project was built over an oil bed. He was planning on sabotaging all of Scripps' research by destroying some of the Bio Domes and getting the Project shut down.

Then he could sell the results of his own experiments for personal profit, and sell the information about the oil bed to the highest bidder.

'He didn't count on there being aliens in the abyss, mind you,' says Martha.

'And he didn't count on the bravery and quick thinking of you and your companions, either,' says Jacques with a twinkle in his eye.

You can see that Scripps feels awfully let down by Jolla — they had, after all, been working together for years. It has pained Scripps to discover the truth about his friend.

You remind Scripps that much of his research has been saved — and the future of the Project is secure for now.

'Where's the Doctor?' says Scripps. 'I must thank him personally.'

Martha chuckles and says, 'He's getting ready to face the United World Council!'

Turn to 57.

52 Inside the seaweed Bio Dome is an area, roughly the size of a football pitch, covered with dark green plants, swaying gently in a simulated tide.

Amongst the seaweed you spot a scientist in what looks like part lab coat and part scuba-diving suit!

Scripps explains, 'You can't go inside a Bio Dome without putting on a Bio Suit — and then passing through the Decontamination Zone. Inside each Dome is a very carefully balanced ecosystem — add any unknown quantity to that and months of study could be wasted!'

'Then what about that crack?' says the Doctor pointing at a hairline crack running up the side of the Bio Dome. 'It seems to be coming from here…' And he traces the fracture down to a gas canister, attached to the side of the Dome.

Scripps is horrified and races the Mini Sub back to the Wet Dock. He sends you all off to the Canteen Pod while he goes to see Jolla — his Chief Engineer — in the Hub.

Turn to 31.

53 | As the Doctor slips out of the Presentation Pod, a woman in a smart suit turns around and grabs you by the shoulder. She has a big grin on her face. She asks you, 'Who was that?'

'Oh, he's a friend of mine,' you say, proudly. 'He's the Doctor.'

'Doctor who?' asks the woman.

'Just the Doctor,' you smile and turn around and walk away. Your head is full of thoughts about the adventure you've just had, and all the crazy stuff you did, the different people you met and the wild things you saw along the way.

You keep smiling as you think of all the choices you had to make, all the quick thinking and everything you had to remember.

And you smile to yourself as you walk all the way back to the TARDIS in Storage Pod E.

Or was it Storage Pod A...?

THE END

54 Believing you to be members of the Ocean Futures Organisation, Scripps — the man in charge of the Project — leads you around the main corridor towards the South Quadrant — the Science Quarter.

On your right hand side are many circular doorways. On the left, round viewing windows afford you tantalising glimpses of the wreck of an old cruise liner.

'Around the world, cities are overcrowded, suburbs sprawl outwards and connecting motorways choke the countryside,' says Scripps. 'Humankind must search for alternative food sources and find a new way of reaping the planet's rich food store. It is time to turn to the oceans!'

You reach the South Quadrant and Scripps leads you into a Laboratory Pod. From here, you can see the Bio Dome field — large plexiglas hemispheres organised in a grid-like fashion — as far as you can see.

Scripps asks you if you'd like to check out a seaweed Bio Dome? Go to 93. Or a shellfish Bio Dome? Go to 58.

Jolla is trying to get his Construction Suit to pick itself back up and carry him to safety. But the machine is like a crab that can't right itself, rolling around on its back on the seabed.

You can see that the cab of Jolla's vehicle is cracked and letting in seawater... Suddenly, the cab implodes. Everyone is shouting to each other over the intercom but you can't make out any particular words.

You think Jolla must have been crushed...

But then you spot him, swimming away towards the abyss! He must have had some of the silver sachets! You're about to tell the others when you realise you can't see him any more... He seems to have disappeared.

How long will the effects of the experimental liquid last? Perhaps someone from Envirocon is waiting for him in the abyss? Who knows...?

But, one thing's for sure — he's had his chips on-board the Corinthian Project!

Mmm... Chips...

Turn to 94.

56 You ask Scripps if he wouldn't mind taking a short detour over the wreck.

'No problem!' he says. 'It's always a tragic and beautiful thing to see.'

As the Sub glides over the sunken ship, you crane your neck to get a better look.

'Looks like you had a near miss when that thing came down,' jokes the Doctor.

'Oh no, the Corinthian Project was built around the wreck of the old Corinthian cruise liner,' says Scripps. You and Martha exchange a look — Scripps might be a nice guy but he obviously doesn't have much of a sense of humour.

'Isn't it kind of macabre to have the Project built around a shipwreck?' Martha asks.

'My grandfather designed the Corinthian,' says Scripps. 'This Project is my tribute to him.'

The Doctor says he wouldn't mind a closer look. Scripps says it's off-limits to visitors.

Turn to 52.

You take a seat alongside Martha and Jacques at the back of the Presentation Pod, just as the Doctor steps up on to the stage at the U.W.C. conference.

Jacques begins to tell you that Jolla has been spotted — alive and well — and is currently being held on a nearby Envirocon vessel. He's not sure what the Envirocon sub was doing in waters around here... but he had no more time to speculate — the Doctor's about to begin his speech!

The Doctor explains to the assembled United World Council about the existence of the Dax, using saved footage from a memory card that he took from Jacques, as evidence. Everyone gasps when they see the aliens — just as you did when you first saw them.

He also mentions the oil field beneath the old Corinthian — but, of course, nobody is very excited about that now.

He says that he hopes the United World Council will work together with the Ocean Futures Organisation to use this knowledge responsibly and in a way that benefits all humankind.

You think about something the Doctor said to you once — and he was right. Knowledge is power. Or rather, withholding knowledge can make you powerful. If everyone knows about the Dax — and the oil field —

then no individual is quite so powerful. And Jolla has lost.

Plus, all of Scripps' hard work was not for nothing. He still has plenty of data left that has not been corrupted or destroyed. Although what everyone will make of his research into seaweed after the Doctor's revelations, is another matter!

The Doctor steps down from the podium to a standing ovation. Afterwards, the room is buzzing. The last thing anyone expected when they were invited to a seminar on the ocean floor was to encounter aliens from outer space!

Turn to 53.

Scripps says he'd be delighted to take you to the shellfish Bio Dome, and he jumps on-board a personal transportation vehicle that looks like a golf buggy. It only has two seats, so you sit next to him.

Meanwhile, the Doctor hops into the driving seat of another cart. The Doctor pats the passenger seat next to him but Martha grins mischievously and climbs into the one remaining buggy.

The electric engine of your vehicle whines as Scripps picks up speed, driving you in a clockwise direction around the circular building.

'The Project is home to just over a hundred pioneers,' Scripps tells you.

It's hard to concentrate on what he is saying as you are aware that the Doctor and Martha are having a race in the other two carts. They speed past you, laughing like naughty kids!

'Each pioneer has given up his or her home comforts to share this under-sea settlement,' Scripps goes on, 'and has dedicated him or herself to exploring a new kind of landscape and cultivating acres of modified strains of nutritious sea life in the Bio Domes... As we're about to see!'

Scripps stops the buggy at the Wet Dock. Martha and the Doctor hurry back on foot, having shot past on their buggies.

Scripps slides up a garage door and what you see inside amazes you all… Large humanoid-shaped vehicles rigged out with grabbing claws, welding gear and other heavyweight equipment. There are four of them — each in its own parking bay.

'Advanced Atmospheric Construction Suits,' grins Scripps. 'Each one has its own abilities. We used them in the construction of the Project. Now they're used for maintenance and in emergencies.'

Martha helps you strap yourself into a Construction Suit. The cab is sealed, so you don't need scuba-gear.

Piloting the A.A.C.S. is easy — the legs and arms of the vehicle move as an extension of your own limbs.

Now head out to the Bio Domes by turning to 47!

59 Flux hits a button. The door seals shut and the airlock begins filling with water.

Flux rips off the top of his sachet and empties the contents into his mouth.

'Come on!' he says, although his mouth sounds like it's full of cotton wool. 'Hurry up!'

The water rises up to your chest. You suck out the contents of your sachet and your mouth fills with a thick, metallic-tasting liquid. It's so foul, you almost spit it right out. But you force yourself to swallow it.

At that moment it occurs to you that are putting all your trust in Flux...

Seawater covers your head. You have no air left in your lungs. There's nothing you can do except swallow seawater... And discover you can breathe underwater!

Flux grins at you and gives you a big thumbs up!

The other side of the airlock bursts open and you swim out into the open ocean. What an amazing sensation!

You swim over to Jolla's Sea Bike just as another explosion rips up the edge of the abyss.

You see that Jolla is looking down at the Doctor and Martha's Mini Sub, which is half buried by rocks, dislodged by the explosions.

You hope that Jolla can't see you in the clouds of debris swirling around.

Flux is shouting something into his face mike, but you can't hear anything since you took off your headphones. Who is he talking to?

There's a shift in the rocks and the Mini Sub is crushed as easily as a tin can.

But what about the Doctor and Martha…? They're swimming around you, laughing! There must have been some oxygen sachets in the Sub, and Flux must have told them over the intercom!

You're so happy to be reunited in this extraordinary situation!

But, as the water clears, you come face to face with Jolla on his Sea Bike…

Turn to 23.

60 Martha follows Scripps back towards the airlock. You walk over to the coral reef, enjoying the powerful strides made by your Construction Suit.

The colours of the coral reef are electric — as though it's illuminated from the inside.

The Doctor suggests you'd better return to the Project — and that's when you realise the right foot of your Suit is fixed into a giant clam.

The Doctor uses the drill bit on his Construction Suit to pierce two hydraulic canisters. The liquids mix and sink down into the giant clam.

The jaws of the clam open up and you can remove your foot. You ask the Doctor what he just did.

He chuckles and says, 'Oh, I just mixed up some drycelonen triclorinate paracyclote.'

You ask what that is.

He says, 'Sneezing powder for clams.'

Now catch up with the others by turning to 31.

You step up on to the back bumper of the buggy and hold on tight. The Doctor puts his foot down hard!

Jolla is speeding around the Project in a clockwise direction and you're in hot pursuit!

You're right behind him when he stops so abruptly that his cart skids and tips over. He stumbles out and over to the door of the Wet Dock.

Jolla waves the weapon at you and warns you to keep your distance. It looks like a water pistol — but you don't want to chance it.

With the weapon in one hand and a fistful of memory cards in the other, Jolla struggles to activate the door.

He gets it open, but drops his weapon.

As you reach the door, it hisses shut in your face.

Go to 33 to wait for the Doctor to unlock the door with the sonic screwdriver. Go to 2 to pick up the weapon.

The sides of the Sub are groaning and start to bend under the pressure. Flux's voice burbles over the intercom. It sounds as though he's underwater. He says, 'Can you hear me?'

'Yes!' cries Martha. 'We're trapped under a landslide and our Sub has sprung a leak!'

'I know,' glugs Flux. 'I'm close by.'

'What do we need to do?' says the Doctor. The water is up round your waist.

'Don't worry, you're not sunk yet,' gurgles Flux. 'Locate the First Aid Kit in the ceiling panel.'

The Doctor rips out the First Aid Kit, as the ceiling begins to buckle down. 'Got it!' he says.

'There are some sachets inside,' burbles Flux. But his voice is breaking up as the intercom disappears under the water. 'Rip them open… Swallow the contents!'

Seawater gushes in. It's up to your chest. The Doctor hands out the sachets. The water's up to your chin. It's now or never with the sachet.

Do you swallow the contents? Turn to 40.
Or take a deep breath and hope for the
best? Turn to 41.

Flux brings out a tray of different sodas for you to try. Martha just wants a glass of water. 'Are you serious?' says, Flux. 'We're under the sea. Where are we going to find drinking water?'

You ask Flux if there's no way of purifying the seawater.

He says, 'Yes, but it's easier to recycle our waste into flavoured drinks.'

Martha spits out a mouthful of 'pineapple juice'. Flux laughs. He says, 'Only joking! All our juices are actually made from different strains of seaweed.'

Martha frowns. 'Seaweed juice? Eurgh! That sounds almost as bad.'

You open a bottle of mango-flavoured juice. It fizzes all over the tray.

'That's strange,' frowns Flux. 'It's not usually fizzy.'

You tighten the lid and slip the bottle into your pocket for later.

'Now you've tried drinking seaweed,' says Flux, 'I think you're ready for a real challenge!'

Turn to 66 to find out what it is.

64 You sneak down to the Wet Dock.

Flux and Marion know the whereabouts of all the scuba-diving equipment. There's enough gear for everyone on-board the Project, but you all think it's better if some of you stay behind and keep an eye out for trouble.

It's agreed that you and the Doctor will go out to the wreck. Luckily, there are headphones and face mikes for everyone. They work well under water, so you can all keep in touch.

You get kitted out with all the gear — snorkel, hood, mask, wetsuit, the lot! It weighs a tonne! Martha laughs as you try to walk in the fins, carrying the weighted belt and oxygen cylinders.

You can hardly stagger down to the airlock but you somehow manage it.

Once you get out into the water, however, it's a different story!

You swim over to the wreck — getting there before the Doctor, who you suspect might not have done that much swimming in his long lifetime!

The ship is split down the middle and the two halves have been crushed into each other. You wonder what caused the ship to sink.

The hull is eroding away and is encrusted with sea life. It looks almost organic, as though it is growing out of the seabed rather than having dropped from the surface.

The Doctor's examining a cabin door with the sonic screwdriver. Hey, you didn't know it worked underwater — but then you never thought to ask.

The deck of the ship is slanting at a crazy angle. You swim over a hatch on the deck. It is closed, just like the cabin door the Doctor is looking at. You pull at the hatch but you can't get it open.

Do you wave the Doctor over to the hatch? Turn to 67. Or do you want to try and open the door? Turn to 68.

You call out to the Doctor, but it's not his voice you hear over your headphones — it's Jolla's!

He says, 'I'm going to get rid of those creepy creatures and these meddling strangers at the same time!' You see Jolla launch something from his Sea Bike...

And an explosion rocks the edge of the abyss!

You cry out! And you hear Jolla say, 'Who's that? Who's there?'

You tear off the headphones and run straight into Flux.

'What's going on?' says Flux, excitedly.

You explain that the Doctor and Martha are investigating the abyss in a Mini Sub — and that Jolla is setting off explosives.

Flux sees you're not joking.

You tell him you're going out in the remaining Sea Bike.

'No,' says Flux. 'Jolla's been tampering with it. Try this instead.' Flux hands you a sachet of liquid.

Turn to 59.

You leave the Canteen Pod with the Doctor and Martha. You follow Flux and Marion into the corridor where they are looking through a small round window. From here you can see out to the wreck of the old Corinthian cruise liner.

'It's amazing, isn't it?' says Marion.

'We dare you to swim out to it,' says Flux.

And the twins turn round to you grinning.

'I'm game,' says the Doctor.

You point out that Scripps said it was out of bounds.

'That makes it even more exciting!' says Martha.

Martha's right. Visiting the wreck could be an adventure!

'You could use the Atmospheric Suits!' says Flux.

'No way,' says Marion. 'They're too obvious. You'd be seen from miles away!'

'Then you've got two choices,' says Flux. 'Scuba-diving suits, or these...' And he holds up a fistful of silver sachets.

Go to 64 to try scuba-diving or turn to 45 to find out what's in those sachets.

67 The Doctor comes over to inspect the hatch. Although it looks like it hasn't been opened in a long time, the Doctor points out where some of the rust has fallen away.

'So much for the wreck being out of bounds,' says the Doctor. 'This hatch has been opened recently!'

You open the hatch. It's dark inside the ship and your torches aren't very bright, as you don't want to draw attention to yourselves.

Nevertheless, you lower yourself down through the hatch to take a look. Inside the hull of the ship, the decks have rotted away... Or maybe they've been removed... Because you can see all the way down to the ocean bed...

And there's some pumping equipment.

'It looks like someone's been looking for oil,' says the Doctor. 'But who?'

You hear a voice on your headphones. It's Flux, calling you back to the Project before you run out of air.

Swim back to 83.

You pull the hatch open but, before you can look into it, the Doctor needs you over at the door.

Behind the rusted up door is a small cabin. It's dark inside — but you can make out some sort of control panel. It looks in pretty good shape compared to the rest of the ship — almost new.

You're about to make a joke about the panel being 'shipshape' when a needle twitches across a dial. You tap the glass with your finger. Hey — the dials are monitoring something!

'Yes,' says the Doctor. 'But what?'

The door slams shut, plunging you into darkness.

You mustn't panic, you don't want to use up all your oxygen. In the blackness you can hear a pulsing sound. You ask the Doctor if he can hear it too.

'It sounds like an oil pump,' says the Doctor. 'Which would explain those control panels.'

You help the Doctor heave open the door.

Flux calls you back to the Project. You're relieved to leave the spooky old ship.

Swim back to 83.

69 | To reach the wreck of the Corinthian cruise liner, you need to go down to the Wet Dock, through the airlock and swim over the Project... Without being spotted.

Still, it should be easier without wearing all that bulky diving gear!

Flux has only got three sachets of the prototype liquid, so you can't all go out to the wreck. Between you, it's decided that the Doctor will stay behind with Marion. He says he'll keep a close eye on you from the Project — and he wants a full report when you get back.

That leaves you, Flux and Martha to try the sachets and swim out to the wreck.

The three of you step into the airlock and rip off the top of your sachets. You watch as Flux drinks down the contents of the sachet. He grimaces. It obviously tastes disgusting.

The Doctor hits the button that activates the airlock and it starts filling with water.

'Go on, you two!' he shouts. Martha looks as nervous as you feel. But she shrugs and downs the sachet.

The water in the airlock is already up to your chest. It's now or never! You throw the contents of the sachet into your mouth and swallow without tasting.

The water rises above your head. You have no air left in your lungs. There's nothing you can do except swallow seawater... And discover that you can breathe underwater!

You look around at Martha and Flux. They are laughing and making for the exterior door as it opens up to the sea.

Swimming underwater without breathing apparatus is a weird sensation. But as soon as you relax and go with it, it feels pretty natural.

Do you want to take a look at the bow of the wreck? Turn to 90. Or the stern? Turn to 72.

You can't all go through the airlock at the same time, so it's agreed that those in the Atmospheric Construction Suits will go out first. The faster vehicles will go second and catch up.

This gives Flux a moment to show you how to pilot the Sea Bike. It looks a bit like a jet ski contained in a clear shell, so you can ride it underwater without a diving suit.

It's your turn to pass through the airlock. It fills with seawater and the exterior doors open up... You can't imagine that this could ever get boring. The coral reef is ahead of you, the abyss is on your left, the Bio Domes are on your right, and above you — who knows! The sea is so full of possibilities!

You twist hard on the accelerator and gun the Sea Bike around to the Bio Domes.

Weaving in and out of the first row, you find the Doctor at the Dome you examined earlier on. He has cleverly attached the sonic screwdriver to a probe on the arm of his Advanced Atmospheric Construction Suit. He is using it to disarm one of the detonators.

Meanwhile, Martha is piloting another A.A.C.S. and striding inbetween the Bio Domes, looking for gas tanks and detonators.

She spots one, and uses the claw-like grab of her Suit to carefully remove the limpet-like detonator from the gas tank. She then tries to articulate the arm of her Suit to flick away the detonator – in the same way as you would try to remove something sticky from the tip of your fingers.

Her idea works... but the detonator shoots through the water and sticks to the shell of your Sea Bike!

You need to get rid of it! Quick!

Do you want to scrape it off on the coral – turn to 91 – or against the edge of the abyss – turn to 82?

71 | You follow the rope into the ship.

It's kind of spooky inside. You hope nobody died when the cruise liner went down. Imagine — one moment you're soaking up the sun up on the deck, the next minute you're being swallowed by the ocean...

No, wait a minute. You're sure that everyone would have escaped. After all, the Titanic didn't have enough lifeboats — a lesson must have been learned from that. Right?

Inside the hull of the ship, the decks have rotted away...or maybe they've been removed...because you can see all the way down to the ocean bed...

And there's some pumping equipment. It's moving — and that's what was jerking the rope.

You wave Martha over to look at the pump.

Flux taps his wrist and winds his index fingers around each other. You guess this means that you haven't got long before whatever was in those sachets wears off.

Swim back to 83.

You swim round to the back of the rusting wreck. You can hardly believe it used to be a luxurious cruise liner. Now look at it. Still. Lifeless.

Wait a minute — that old propeller there seems to be moving. It is moving! Slowly — but moving nonetheless.

Maybe the wreck is haunted!

No, wait a minute! It's being turned by a deep sea current. You can feel it, almost as though it's pushing you away from the wreck. As though there's something there you shouldn't see.

You look inside the hull of the cruise liner. It's dark inside, but you can clearly see some pumping equipment. The propeller is driving it.

Flux taps his wrist and jerks his thumb back in the direction of the airlock. You guess this means that the sachets are about to wear off and you'd better get back.

Swim back to 83.

You come together with everyone else in the South Quadrant.

All of you are out of breath from running around the Project. But no one has seen Jolla.

Suddenly, you're drenched in water, as though someone has thrown a full bucket of water over you.

You all look up. The sprinklers have come on.

'Hel-lo!' shouts Martha, to no one in particular. 'I already took a shower today!' She wipes wet hair out of her eyes.

You're all soaking and the water bounces off the floor, around your feet.

'Jolla has been tampering with the Project's emergency systems,' yells Scripps, over the wail of the fire alarm and the rushing sound of the sprinklers. 'He's used to controlling everything from the Hub. He could have sabotaged the whole place!'

'That's it!' shouts the Doctor, over the wail of the siren. 'The siren and the sprinklers — they're just a distraction. There are still explosives on the Bio Domes!'

'Explosives?' gasps Scripps.

'They're only very small explosives,' shouts the Doctor. 'But they're attached to gas cylinders! The plan is to explode them. It will look like a careless accident — as though a build up of gas in the Bio Domes has gone unchecked.'

'Has he gone crazy?' yells Scripps. 'Releasing those modified crops into the open sea could be a disaster for the environment! This could be a catastrophe on a global scale!'

'I don't think Jolla cares much about that,' says the Doctor. 'I think he just wants to make his money!'

You all need to get out there and disarm those explosives!

'We can go out in the Construction Suits,' says Scripps. 'But we have to get back to the North Quad!'

If you have just seen Flux using a Construction Suit, then you know there is one close by and you can turn to 84. Otherwise (or if you'd rather stick with the group) follow the others to 4.

Flux glares at you as you confess that you went out to the wreck for a dare... But before Scripps can get too mad at you, you jump in with information of your discovery: someone is using the Project as a base while they search the seabed for oil!

'And that same person,' says the Doctor, 'could be planning on sabotaging the Bio Domes.'

'Why would anyone do that?' Scripps wants to know.

'To discredit your research,' says the Doctor, 'or cause chaos at tomorrow's presentation. Either way, if the funding is cut, then the Project will be closed down — and then the land can be sold off for personal profit. And if the land happened to be sitting on an oil bed...'

'Then it would be worth loads of money,' says Flux as he suddenly understands what the Doctor has been getting at.

The Doctor says, 'What do you think, Jolla?'

You all turn around to face Jolla and he's holding some sort of weapon. It looks like a water pistol, but none of you want to chance it. He backs out of the room.

'I don't know who you are,' says Jolla to the Doctor, 'but I don't like you at all.'

And the door of the Hub slides closed between them.

You glance around the room and share a look with everyone. And then the Doctor springs into action!

He activates the door and runs into the corridor. You're right behind him and Martha is close behind you. There's no sign of Jolla.

'Shouldn't we split up?' says Martha. 'The Project is like a circle — if we go our separate ways, we're bound to intercept Jolla going one way or the other.'

She's right!

If you want to go clockwise, with Martha, turn to 81. If you'd rather go anti-clockwise, with the Doctor, turn to 92.

Flux and Marion aren't too keen on climbing up through the hatch — but they don't mind giving you a leg up. Martha reaches down and helps pull you into the roof space where a maze of pipes and a mess of cables control the atmosphere throughout the Project.

You wave goodbye to Flux and Marion and slide the hatch closed. It's dark now, and cramped.

You follow Martha, who is close behind the Doctor. He's spotted Jacques through an air conditioning vent.

The air up here is hot and dusty. It's hard to breath. You stifle a cough.

Crawling over the cables, you discover that some of the pipes are hot when you lean against one and it burns against the small of your back.

There seems to be two clear ways to go from here. The Doctor asks you which way you think you should go.

To go left, turn to 29. To go right, turn to 27.

76 | **S**uddenly the door hisses closed behind you and the lock collapses into place.

Apart from a dim, green glow from an emergency alarm panel, the room is pitch dark. It's not enough for you to explore Jolla's Pod and look for anything incriminating. It's not even enough to stop you walking smack into Martha.

'Ow!' she says, as you tread on her foot. 'Careful!'

You sit on the edge of Jolla's desk enjoying the peace and quiet when the humming stops. Now it really is silent. Deadly silent.

You've become so used to the humming of the atmosphere generator you'd stopped noticing it. You marvel at the silence for a moment, before realising what it means. Jolla has shut off the air to his Pod.

Three people could use up all the oxygen, in a Pod this size, in a matter of hours.

Jolla's after you, and he thinks he's got you trapped... but he hasn't accounted for the Doctor's sonic screwdriver!

You break out to 79.

You suddenly remember something — the explosive mango-flavoured seaweed drink from the canteen! You check your pocket.

The soda bottle's still there, so you take it out. It's sticky and covered with pocket fluff. You give it a good shake and hope for the best...

You turn the lid... or, at least you try to. Why did you screw it on so tightly?

Smoke's beginning to fill the room. The Doctor's trying to salvage the memory cards while Martha runs around looking for an extinguisher.

You grip the lid on the soda bottle so hard that it chafes the palm of your hand as you twist the bottle and then...

With a loud hiss it starts to spray — all over you. You chuck the bottle into the filing cabinet and the spray of sticky juice extinguishes the flames.

'Well done, you!' says the Doctor, taking a half-melted memory card out of the charred cabinet — and then dropping it because it's hot. 'Oooh — ow!'

Turn to 73.

78 | As everyone assembles at the Wet Dock, there's a scramble for sea able vehicles.

There are three Atmospheric Construction Suits, a couple of Sea Bikes, a Mini Sub and scuba-diving gear. But, of course, there's always the chance that any of this stuff could have been sabotaged by Jolla…

You ask Scripps about the silver sachets with the stuff inside that enables you to breathe underwater.

'How do you know about those?' Scripps asks.

You shrug and say you overheard a couple of people talking about them. Flux gives you a hard stare.

'We have been developing something like that but, as yet, it's totally untested and we don't even know if it works,' says Scripps. 'There could be terrible side effects.'

Now it's your turn to give Flux a hard stare!

Do you want to head out in a Construction Suit? Go to 95. Or on a Sea Bike? Turn to 70.

Back in the corridor, the Doctor grins — he's holding a file with one word across the front: Envirocon.

'How did you find that?' asks Martha, incredulous. 'In the dark, and so quickly!'

'I'm good at finding things people don't want me to see,' says the Doctor.

You ask him what he thinks is in the file.

'It's all here,' he says. 'Everything we need to link Jolla with a global oil company.'

'So it's Jolla who is looking for oil,' says Martha.

'Exactly,' says the Doctor. 'And I think he's sabotaged the Bio Domes as well.'

You ask why.

'To discredit Scripps' research,' says the Doctor. 'You see, if tomorrow's presentation goes badly, then the Project could be closed down. Leaving the oil bed free to be exploited by —'

'Envirocon,' finishes Martha.

'Exactly,' says the Doctor.

Suddenly, a loud alarm goes off and an automated voice instructs everyone to evacuate the West Quadrant.

Turn to 86.

Smoke's beginning to fill the room. The Doctor's trying to salvage the memory cards.

You can't believe that there isn't a fire extinguisher close to hand.

'And how come the sprinklers haven't come on?' Martha wants to know.

Over the top of the fire siren you hear a steady series of crashes. They're getting louder.

You double over, coughing from the smoke. And when you look up... there's an Advanced Atmospheric Construction Suit towering in the doorway!

The huge suit of automated body armour, more suited to underwater construction work, moves through the smoke and stomps over to the fire. It sways about a bit, before steadying itself... and training a jet of water on the fire!

Once the fire is safely out, the cab pops open – and there's Flux, grinning away!

'Nice one, Flux!' says Martha, and she gives him a high five as he jumps down from the cab of the A.A.C.S.

Turn to 73.

81 | You follow Martha as she takes a right out of the Hub. You are both running round the Project in a clockwise direction — towards the East Quadrant, the Social Quarter.

You race past the Canteen Pod, Accommodation Pods and Recreation Pods. You look for Jolla everywhere you go. You see people drinking tea and chatting. You see people exercising in the gym and surfing the net for news from the surface.

They're all doing normal stuff, unaware that one of their most senior staff is hoping to destroy their hard work — for his short-term personal gain.

Suddenly, a loud alarm goes off. It makes you jump.

'What does that mean?' says Martha.

A loud automated voice answers her question. It says, 'Fire hazard in the West Quadrant. Please proceed calmly to your designated emergency assembly point.'

You keep on running towards the Science Quarter.

   Turn to 73.

You speed over to where the seabed slopes down into the abyss. There are plenty of jagged rocks there that look as though they might be suitable for prizing the detonator away from your Sea Bike before it explodes!

You don't like the look of the black water down below. You would hate to lose power and drift down there...

It takes some clever driving but you manage to ditch the detonator — and just in time! It goes off and blows up a great chuck of rock, which tumbles down the side of the abyss.

You can't be sure but, for a moment, you think you see something moving down there, something more than just falling rock.

You head up and out of the abyss. You turn towards the Bio Domes... and come face to face with Jolla!

He's piloting one of the Construction Suits — the biggest, toughest-looking one of them all. He takes a swing at you with one of the heavy tools attached to the arm of the Suit.

It smashes into the shell of your Sea Bike and cracks shoot across the plexiglas. Luckily, the shell holds, but you don't think it could withstand a second hit.

Jolla swings back the arm of the suit. He's going to take a second pop at you. He is so focussed on destroying your Bike that he is unaware of a shadow falling across him.

The Doctor is right behind him and drawing back the arm of his Construction Suit.

The two heavy, powerful vehicles smash into one another!

You use the moment to power the Sea Bike out of danger.

Meanwhile, Jolla takes a swing at the Doctor.

The Doctor blocks Jolla's attack and sends a spinning saw blade into a power cable at the knee joint of his vehicle.

The leg of Jolla's vehicle locks and the whole thing topples over onto the seabed.

Turn to 55.

83 Back at the Wet Dock, you discuss what you've seen. It's seems that someone is checking the area around the Project for oil...

'But who?' asks Marion. 'The whole point of the Corinthian Project is that we're trying to find renewable energy sources — not go looking for reserves of fossil fuels to burn!'

You head over to the Hub to meet up with Scripps — to see what he's found out about the devices you spotted earlier, out at the Bio Domes.

The Hub is situated in the Service Quarter of the Corinthian Project. It is not at the centre of the building, but you can see that it is at the centre of everything that goes on.

You can hear the click and whir of hard discs being overwritten as computers back up the data that's being streamed over from the Laboratory Pods. Banks of TV screens monitor what's happening around the whole building, via discreetly placed cameras (you don't remember seeing any cameras since you arrived).

Scripps is waiting for you — along with a man with a scowling face below neatly parted blonde hair. This is Jolla — the Chief Engineer of the Project.

As the Doctor greets Scripps with a smile and a handshake, you start to wonder if there's a camera or two fixed on the old wreck… This question is answered for you…

Before Scripps can fill you in on the devices, Jolla suddenly notices something on one of the monitors.

'Someone has been out to the old Corinthian,' he says. You look at the monitor over his shoulder and it shows an image of the wreck… and a hatch on the deck has been left open! Jolla is furious.

To confess, turn to 74. To bluff, turn to 25.

84 You leave the others and run, through the sprinkler-drenched corridor, back to the West Quadrant.

You arrive at the still smouldering Study Pod and there it is… the Atmospheric Construction Suit that Flux used to put out the fire!

You climb up into the pilot seat and seal the cab.

And then you realise… you can't just march out of the building… Well, you probably could smash through the wall in this powerful vehicle… but that would flood the whole Project!

There are emergency airlocks in case of emergencies — but they're only big enough to pass through wearing scuba-gear.

There's nothing else to do except stomp around to the Wet Dock.

You stagger around the main corridor of the Project, trying not to do too much damage with the massive crunching feet and tool-loaded arms of the Suit.

Everyone is surprised to see you turn up at the Wet Dock in the A.A.C.S.! You hop down from the cab and join the others.

Go to 78.

Taking seats at the back, you try not to be distracted by the shadows of sea creatures passing by the glass dome as you listen to the welcome speeches.

You find out that the TARDIS has taken the Doctor, Martha and yourself forward in time and deposited you on-board the Corinthian Project — an experimental community on the ocean floor. The Ocean Futures Organisation — or O.F.O. — a charitable organisation dedicated to furthering our understanding of the seas, is funding the work being done on the Project.

There are over a hundred permanent residents here and their mission is to see if humans can live on the seabed, without damaging the environment. Any other discoveries that are made — in the fields of biology, ecology, anthropology or engineering — are to be exploited for the benefit of humankind.

The Corinthian Project itself is a loop. Around the loop are various locations, or Pods. In the centre of the loop is the wreck of a luxury liner called the Corinthian. This serves as a reminder to all of the folly of 'building big' and using the ocean's resources solely for personal pleasure.

Scripps, the Project Manager, is hosting a United World Council summit tomorrow. Scripps is to give a big presentation, demonstrating the social and scientific successes of the project. The U.W.C. give money to the O.F.O. — so it's a very important presentation!

Luckily for you and your companions, it looks as though you can pass for visiting members of the O.F.O. for the duration of your stay. And with a futuristic, experimental, underwater community to explore, it's going to be an exciting couple of days!

As you file out of the Presentation Pod, the Doctor collars Scripps and asks him for a personal tour of the Project.

Turn to 54 to witness the wonder of the Bio Domes. If you want to experience the thrills of the Wet Dock, go to 7.

'The West Quadrant!' says the Doctor. 'Come on!'

As you race towards the West Quadrant, you come across people walking quickly in the other direction. They are all talking about a fire.

You question the logic of running towards the fire. The Doctor says, 'It's the Study Quarter! All the Archives are there.'

'I get it,' says Martha, 'Jolla's trying to destroy all the records — the results of all the research!'

'That's right,' says the Doctor.

Security shutters are coming down to block your way into the West Quadrant, but the Doctor dives underneath them. You and Martha follow.

You enter an Archive Pod. Inside, the ventilation grill is struggling to process the thick black smoke that's coming out of one of the filing cabinets as the memory cards burn inside.

All three of you start coughing.

Did you try a soda in the canteen? If so, turn to 77. If not, turn to 80.

87 You take a seat on the back row of the Presentation Pod. The Doctor and Martha are sitting on your left, and your new friends Flux and Marion slip into the empty seats on your right. They are both grinning.

'I think they're a bit in awe of you,' whispers Martha. 'You piloted your vehicle like a pro!'

The Pod is buzzing, but everyone settles down as Scripps takes to the stage to do his presentation.

Scripps slips comfortably into his spiel about the overcrowded cities and the unexplored oceans... But the Doctor nudges you. It's time to go.

You sneak out and head towards the Storage Pods where you started your adventure.

You've had such a thrilling time on-board the Corinthian Project, you wish you could go back in time and do it all again. Of course, if you did, there are definitely some things you would do differently... Wouldn't you?

THE END

Flux and Marion are speeding around the Bio Domes on the Sea Bikes, while Scripps oversees everything from the Mini Sub.

Your A.A.C.S. takes strong, powerful strides as you pilot it effortlessly over to the coral reef.

Once again, you marvel at the wonder of the reef. Who would want to destroy such an amazing place, just to dredge up a limited supply of oil?

There are all kinds of hollows and grottos where Jolla could hide out here if he was just wearing scuba-gear. But then a thought occurs to you... there were three Construction Suits, but weren't there four parking bays...?

Then Martha calls your name across the intercom!

You turn round and you see that Jolla is wearing the fourth A.A.C.S. – and he's using it to attack Martha! The two heavy vehicles smash into one another.

Jolla's Suit is powerful, but Martha's reflexes are faster. Jolla's vehicle smashes down on the seabed.

Turn to 55.

Your A.A.C.S. takes strong, powerful strides as you pilot it further down the Bio Dome field, keeping a sharp eye out for anything suspicious.

You see something moving rapidly just behind you. You spin round and it's Flux on a Sea Bike, speeding over to assist the Doctor.

When you turn back, you're face to face with Jolla. And he's wearing an Atmospheric Construction Suit — just the same as yours.

He swings a heavy lifting grab at the cab of your Suit. Instinctively, you move your hand. The arm of your vehicle shoots up and blocks his attack.

Good job your reflexes are sharp — those hours spent playing computer games weren't wasted!

Your block throws Jolla off balance and you use the opportunity to kick out at the back of one of Jolla's vehicle's two legs.

Jolla's A.A.C.S. smashes down on the ocean floor, sending up a cloud of sand.

Turn to 55.

You swim around to the front of the wreck. It's an amazing sight — all rusting away and covered by cockles and seaweed, as though the seabed is trying to claim it.

You're careful not to scratch yourself on the sharp edges of the rusting metal. If you did that, you might bleed a little into the water... and wouldn't that attract sharks?

Sharks! You never thought about that! Still, it's a bit late to start worrying about sharks now!

You feel something touch your ankle. You pull your foot away but it only tightens its grip!

You look down and see your foot is tangled up in a rope!

You manage to shake it off, but something is pulling at the end of the rope.

Do you want to follow the rope through a hole in the bow of the ship? Turn to 71. Or ditch the rope and check out the stern? Turn to 72.

You scoot over to the coral reef. There are plenty of jagged edges where you might be able to scrape off the detonator — before it explodes and cracks the shell of your Sea Bike!

It takes some skilful driving but you manage to lose the detonator — and just in time! It goes off and blows up a great chuck of coral. Scripps is going to be furious with you! But at least the Bio Domes are all in one piece and no mutant strains of seaweed are going to be washed into the open sea!

Suddenly, Martha calls your name across the intercom.

You turn away from the reef and see that Jolla is piloting a Construction Suit — and he's using it to attack Martha! The two heavy vehicles smash into one another.

Jolla's Suit is powerful, but Martha's reflexes are faster. Jolla's vehicle smashes down on the seabed.

Turn to 55.

92 You follow the Doctor as he takes a left out of the Hub. You are both running round the Project in an anticlockwise direction — towards the West Quadrant, the Study Quarter.

You race past Storage Pods, Archive Pods and Study Pods. You can't see Jolla anywhere — but you do see men and women taking books down from the shelves and reading. For some reason, it reassures you that, in this future civilisation of amazing automated body armour and space age food, people still feel the need to read books.

It also makes you feel better that, in all this craziness, normal life still carries on here — not that it will for much longer, if Jolla gets his way.

You're jerked out of the moment by a loud siren.

An automated voice instructs you to leave the West Quadrant and so you both keep running to the Science Quarter.

Turn to 73.

Back in the main corridor, Scripps leads you towards the seaweed Bio Dome. You continue in a clockwise direction until you've almost done a full circuit of the Project.

'Of course, the idea of harvesting the spoils of the seas is nothing new!' Scripps continues. 'For all time humans have lived on or near coastlines. But what lies deeper under the water? The ocean bed!'

'The interconnected world oceans cover 71 per cent of our planet's surface,' says Martha.

'That's right!' says Scripps. 'And that's a great deal of unharvested Earth!'

Scripps leads you round to the Wet Dock, where you all climb on-board a Mini Sub.

The Sub slides down a ramp and into an airlock, which fills with water.

Scripps pilots the Sub out of the Project and around to the Bio Domes.

If you want to take a look at the wreck of the Corinthian, turn to 56. If you'd rather head straight for the Bio Domes, turn to 52.

94 You and Martha are sharing a plate of chips in the Canteen Pod. You know that the chips are not made from potatoes, but from some other strange sea vegetable — but, right now, they taste like the best chips you've ever eaten!

You try not to drop seaweed relish down the clothes that Scripps has lent you for the United World Council summit. They're a bit on the large side, but they're better than the overalls Flux offered to let you borrow!

The Doctor is sipping a drink through a straw.

'I never thought I'd say this,' he says, 'but I could get used to these seaweed shakes!'

As you tuck in, people keep coming over to all three of you to congratulate you on saving the Bio Domes, protecting all their hard work and securing their future. Perhaps even securing a better future for the world...

Flux and Marion enter and tell you it's time to assemble in the Presentation Pod.

Turn to 87.

95 You can't all go through the airlock at the same time, so it's agreed that those in the Atmospheric Construction Suits will go out first, and the faster vehicles will go second and catch up.

You, the Doctor and Martha all stand side by side in the airlock, each of you sealed into the cab of an awesome A.A.C.S.

The exterior door of the airlock opens up and you walk around to the Bio Domes.

The Doctor goes straight to the Bio Dome you examined earlier on. He has cleverly attached the sonic screwdriver to a probe on the arm of his Suit, and uses it to disarm one of the detonators.

You and Martha look out for other detonators, while keeping an eye out for Jolla.

If you want to look for Jolla at the coral reef, turn to 88. If you'd rather keep searching further down the Bio Dome field, turn to 89.

You look at the sheet of paper. This is what it says:

Welcome to the Corinthian Project! Whether you're a diehard lubber or an experienced sea dweller, please take a moment to look over this list of some of the fascinating things, people and acronyms you may hear about during your stay. The list is, of course, far from comprehensive — so, if in doubt, please don't be afraid to ask any of our friendly Pioneers!

A.A.C.S. — Advanced Atmospheric Construction Suit. Powered body armour, piloted by the wearer. Used in the construction and the maintenance of the Project.

Airlock — to exit the Project into the ocean, you must pass through an airlock.

Bio Dome — mini ecosystems, developing alternative food and energy sources, encapsulated in large, plexiglas hemispheres on the ocean bed.

Bio Dome fields — the grid-like layout of the Bio Domes.

Bio Suit — worn by scientists working inside the Bio Domes to prevent contamination.

Corinthian, The — the sunken cruise liner at the centre of the Project.

Corinthian Project, The — a futuristic, experimental undersea community and multi-disciplinary research facility, created by the O.F.O. and paid for by the U.W.C.

Decontamination Zone — you must visit this area prior to entering a Bio Dome or subsequent to exploring unknown territories.

Dry rack — this is where the Sea Bikes are stored, charged and maintained.

Hub, the — the centre of operations.

Jacques — Senior Manager, and Scripps' father.

Jolla — Chief Engineer.

Mini Sub — a four-seater undersea vehicle.

O.F.O — Ocean Futures Organisation.

Pioneers — people who live on the Project, as opposed to Lubbers — who don't!

Pod — a room, or a space, used for a specific purpose e.g. Canteen Pod, Study Pod.

Scripps — Project Manager, the man in charge!

Sea Bike — single passenger undersea transportation, fast and manoeuvrable.

U.W.C. — United World Council.

Wet Dock — the Pod from which you launch the Sea Bikes.

Now you've collected this list, you can look over it at any time. If you do though, be careful not to lose your place in time and space!

Now, head back to 32 and choose a new direction.

Don't miss these other exciting adventures with the Doctor!

1. Spaceship Graveyard
2. Alien Arena
3. The Time Crocodile
4. The Corinthian Project

Coming soon...

5. The Crystal Snare
6. War of the Robots
7. Dark Planet
8. The Haunted Wagon Train